LAST RUN

BY R. A. MONTGOMERY

ILLUSTRATED BY FRANK BOLLE

BANTAM BOOKS
NEW YORK • TORONTO • LONDON • SYDNEY • AUCKLAND

RL4, age 10 and up

LAST RUN

A Bantam Book/November 1994

*CHOOSE YOUR OWN ADVENTURE® is a registered
trademark of Bantam Books,
a division of Bantam Doubleday Dell Publishing Group, Inc.
Registered in U.S. Patent and Trademark Office and elsewhere.*

*Original conception of Edward Packard
Cover art by Samson Pollen
Interior illustrations by Frank Bolle*

ISBN 0-553-56394-7

Published simultaneously in the United States and Canada

*Bantam Books are published by Bantam Books, a division of
Bantam Doubleday Dell Publishing Group, Inc. Its trademark,
consisting of the words "Bantam Books" and the portrayal of a
rooster, is Registered in U.S. Patent and Trademark Office and
in other countries. Marca Registrada. Bantam Books, 1540
Broadway, New York, New York 10036.*

PRINTED IN THE UNITED STATES OF AMERICA

OPM   0 9 8 7 6 5 4 3 2 1

LAST RUN

WARNING!!!

Do not read this book straight through from beginning to end. These pages contain many different adventures you may have once you hit the slopes of the Italian Dolomites. From time to time as you read along, you will be asked to make a choice. Your choice may lead to success or disaster!

Think carefully before you choose. The adventures you have are the results of your choices. You are responsible because you choose. After you make a decision, follow the instructions to find out what happens to you next.

Though you're eager to make tracks in the investigation of your uncle's murder, you can't help being thrilled about the fabulous skiing you'll get to do. But be extra careful. Even if you do manage the hairy twists and jumps, your skiing skills might not be what it takes to face these slopes. Remember you're in the company of dangerous suspects and ruthless murderers. Skiing might be your expertise, international intrigue is theirs.

Good luck!

You can barely breathe. Snow crystals from the rotor blades of the copter fill the air, and despite your ducking down and covering your mouth and nose with the collar of your parka, the snow crystals have their way. But then the copter is up and gone, and you can breathe again. Far below you in the valley is Corvarra, Italy, a small town tucked away in the Italian Dolomites on the far side of the Alps.

"Well, let's do it!" you yell to no one. With a push you are over the small lip of the cornice, airborne for less than two seconds. Then your skis hit the light powder snow, about eight inches deep over a firm base. It is spring, and the ski season is drawing to a close, but the helicopter skiing and the upper slopes served by a giant tram are still excellent. This is your first run.

But your main reason for being here isn't just the fabulous skiing—it's crime. Two people have been murdered, and the suspicion is that their deaths are linked to twenty-eight million dollars that has disappeared from accounts in two Swiss banks and one Liechtenstein bank. Four suspects in the crime, identified by a private detective agency in London, are gathered in the elegant Golf Hotel, once a hunting lodge for an Austro-Hungarian prince, and the hotel where you are now staying.

Turn to page 2.

2

Your favorite uncle, Gustav Hendrikson, is one of the victims. His death, caused by a hit-and-run driver in Amsterdam, Holland, was suspicious from the start—part of the twenty-eight million dollars was his. That same day, a woman named Inga Maidorf was also mysteriously murdered. There seems to be no known link between her and your uncle, except that a receipt for a six-million-dollar deposit into the same bank apparently used by Uncle Gustav was found in her handbag. Whether this is only a coincidence or not, Uncle Gustav's wife, Isabella Hendrikson, has begged you to seek out the truth and find the killers for her. The police in Holland and Switzerland seem to have hit only dead ends in the case. Maybe someone "big" has paid them off.

"Why me?" you asked Aunt Isabella over the phone when she called to ask you to investigate. You have often spent your summer vacations with her and Uncle Gustav at their home in Zurich, Switzerland, but you have never made that long trip during spring break.

"Because you are the only one I can trust, and because you are very bright and talented," was her reply.

Go on to the next page.

"Well, I'm barely an adult—and hardly experienced in investigating crimes," you told her.

"Precisely the point," she said. "No one will suspect you. You will appear merely as a student on spring holiday. I will send you to the Golf Hotel in Corvarra, Italy. Your skiing talents have been noted in the ski racing circles in Europe as well as the U.S., so you have the perfect cover. I'd come along but I must stay here to work with the police. They need my help following other major leads."

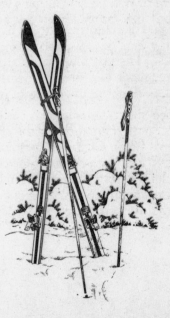

Turn to page 53.

4

"Well done, my young friend. We could really use you in our business," Siegfried says. He takes your hand and leads you ever so cautiously to the doorway. The coast is clear, and the two of you exit and walk quickly to the heart of the small town.

"Here, we might be safe here," Siegfried says, leading you to a small café.

Not another café, you think to yourself. But this one is quaint and completely deserted. The clerk at the counter nods and points to a table in the back room.

"I thought we would be safe in the other place, and that didn't turn out to be true, did it?" he says. "Perhaps here we will have some time to ourselves." His last few words are drowned out by the *bleep bleep* of police cars speeding by, headed no doubt to the scene of mayhem in the rough café.

"What's going on?" you demand as you follow him. Fear has left you, replaced by a current of determination tinged with anger.

"You, my young friend, are the subject of much concern to many people."

"Why me?"

Turn to page 62.

You finally get some rest.

Riinnnng! Riinnnng!

The telephone next to your bed breaks into your thoughts with a harsh, loud bell. You jump up from the bed and approach the telephone warily.

"Hello," you say.

There is silence on the instrument: no voice, no breathing, no mechanical clicking, just silence.

"Who is this?" you demand. More silence, then a click and the sound of the desk clerk asking, "May I help you?"

"No, no. Sorry, wrong number" is your reply.

As you move slowly and thoughtfully back to your desk, your eye is caught by a piece of white paper protruding from beneath your door. You pick it up. Your name is written in a beautiful hand in purple ink. Opening it, you find a cream-colored card with the following message:

> Please be so kind as to join us tomorrow for a ski tour and picnic. We will leave promptly at 7:30 A.M. We have never met, but we assure you that our company will delight you.
>
> Friends of Gustav

Turn to page 34.

6

Twenty-three years later, as you lie in the sun next to the swimming pool on your estate in Greece, you remember that day in the Italian Alps when your future was determined. You are not proud of what you have been and what you have done, but you believe that you have had little or no choice. You reach for a glass of freshly squeezed orange juice. At that very moment, two helicopters drop out of the sky. They are crammed with uniformed police. One of the copters jounces to the ground not ten yards from where you lie.

Turn to page 105.

SOBOLDT AGENCY
CONFIDENTIAL HENDRIKSON cont.
Accident and Autopsy Report
Amsterdam, Holland

At 10:22 P.M. on February 22 a Mr. G. Hendrikson of Copenhagen, Denmark, Passport No. 33.45.789 was found in the center of Amsterdam on Amstel Street and De Magere Bridge.

Mr. Hendrikson was DOA at the Central Hospital Emergency Ward.

Two witnesses reported the same information: a black Mercedes Benz touring car of 1950s origin hit Mr. Hendrikson head-on and did not stop. The car was showing no running lights, and the two people were unable to see any license plate.

One of the witnesses, an American by the name of Michael Durfey, age 26, a medical student on vacation, gave immediate assistance including CPR but to no avail.

Go on to the next page.

Autopsy revealed that Hendrikson died of massive internal injuries including ruptured spleen, fractured thoracic and lumbar vertebrae, and multiple skull fractures. He had also suffered serious abrasions of the face and arms.

Review of blood and stomach samples indicated a high level of a tranquilizer substance found in prescription drugs: Nembutal.

Two computer diskettes were found in the pocket of the overcoat, but both diskettes were blank, seemingly erased.

Within moments of the accident, subject's wife, one Isabella Hendrikson, called the Amsterdam police reporting that her husband was overdue by four hours at a restaurant where they were to have dinner. She identified the body.

Turn to page 44.

10

You decide to go ahead and have a look at the package. You are a sucker for gifts: Christmas, birthdays, any old time. You really like to get them; half the fun is guessing what is in the box. This is well-known to your family; the gift is probably just Aunt Isabella being nice.

The door opens on well-oiled hinges. The corridor is empty, long, sunlit, and elegant. The green carpet is thick and luxurious—a perfect setting for a large basket of fruit and candy wrapped in cellophane.

You are a little disappointed. You would have preferred a package to unwrap. Who wants a bunch of grapefruit and some moldy peaches anyway? But you pick up the basket and bring it into your room. There is a card stuck between the grapes and the bananas. You reach for it.

That's odd. The card is blank. There is also a box of fine chocolates from the chocolate store just next to the hotel. You hope there are chocolate-covered cherries in the box.

Turn to page 37.

12

"So, my young friend, you made it down safely! Good for you. Not everyone would have escaped the White Death so easily. I watched," he says to you, holding out a pair of very expensive-looking Zeiss binoculars to prove his point. "Yes, you are handy on skis. I hope you are as handy on your feet. Danger lurks in high places." He smiles and takes a sip of the steaming brew.

"Thanks," you reply, bending down to pick up your skis. Their new design combines the best performance aspects of high speed racing giant-slalom skis with the quick-turning versatility of an extreme ski, built for the tortures of almost vertical descents. This pair is an experimental design, given to you by a ski company that sponsors you during the racing season. They certainly served you well today, you think.

"I am Siegfried von Holtzgraf, and pleased to meet you." The man holds out his hand and shakes yours with surprising firmness. The smile makes his face look almost cherubic. Your instinct is to like him—but beware, you remind yourself.

The chop-chop-chop of a helicopter punches holes in the calm. Your eyes scan the sky, finding the small speck close to where you started the morning's run.

Turn to page 39.

The trip to the train in Trento is exhausting and without relief. But finally you are aboard and on your way. Gerard waves you off, and you wonder about him. He refused to answer all questions about himself, but you feel that his dedication to getting you safely away has something to do with the death of Inga Maidorf in Rome. He gives you the name and telephone number of a man to contact in Rome. Coincidentally the man turns out to be Siegfried von Holtzgraf, and you arrange to meet him the next day at a small café in the heart of town.

Turn to page 62.

"Thank you very much, Mr. Holtzgraf," you say, "but I'm afraid that I must decline. Perhaps we could meet some other time. I would love to talk with you. Why don't you call me later today?"

"Yes, that would be fine." Siegfried gives a small bow and waddles off.

Shouldering your skis, poles in hand, you are about to head back to the hotel, a mere thirty yards away, when the old man who operates the kiosk says to you in a heavy Italian accent, "That man is a prince. Do not forget it."

"A what?" you ask.

"A prince—of the once-famous Hungarian royal family. He is to be respected."

"Thanks for telling me," you reply, and head off.

The helicopter noise is louder, and finally the craft dips into view, hovers, and touches down. Two people in dark ski clothes climb out without closing the door of the cabin. They duck to clear the slowly rotating blades and hurry away. The copter immediately leaves.

Turn to page 54.

"I'd love to join you for breakfast. But first let me drop off my skis and change," you say to Siegfried.

"Fine, fine. Why don't we meet in the lobby of the Golf in about half an hour? Okay with you?"

"Great. See you soon." As you turn to head toward the hotel, you realize you might have a moment to take a glimpse at the files before you meet Siegfried. You quicken your step.

With a rush of cold air from the outside, you enter the lobby of your hotel. It's warm, and you can't wait to unload all your stuff. As you make your way to the elevator, you hear, "Pardon, pardon!" Again, "Pardon, pardon!" Instinctively you turn and realize a bellboy is calling to you.

"Please. Here is a letter for you," he says with a strong Italian accent. He hands you an envelope. You wonder whom it could possibly be from—probably Aunt Isabella. You turn it over and see that it is addressed to one R. Dunbarton. A look of disappointment crosses your face.

"I'm sorry, but this isn't for me. You've got the wrong person," you explain.

The bellboy looks confused. "But you are not a friend of Isabella Hendrikson? A man said to give it to you."

Go on to the next page.

"Well, Isabella Hendrikson is my aunt. But I'm afraid you've mistaken me for someone else." You hand the letter back. Just then you think to yourself, maybe this R. Dunbarton is involved in your uncle's case. Important clues could be escaping your hands at this very moment. Should you take the letter? Too late—the bellboy grabs and pockets it. "Sorry for the bother," he says, and turns away.

Crime is no easy task: another lesson learned. You promise yourself to be more alert with Siegfried. Oh, I've got to shake a leg! you realize. You don't want to keep Siegfried waiting. But valuable time has been wasted. There's no time to check the files. You hurry to your room and quickly change.

Turn to page 49.

18

Best to be on guard, you think. You reach for the disc, slip it into the machine, and let it boot. Then you open the file and review what is there:

*SIEGFRIED VON HOLTZGRAF   [89]
*CHIN LEE   [22]
*ARTE FUNK   [26]
*DOMINIQUE PASCAL   [30]
*LOCKED FILE—ACCESS **X COMMAND** CODE
    REQUIRED   [42]
*GUSTAV HENDRIKSON & ASSOC.   [79]

*Choose a file to survey by going
to the page number indicated
next to the file name.
Do this now. Review all the files.*

*When you are finished,
turn to page 36.*

You remember your uncle having told you about payoffs to government officials in Japan, the U.S., and Germany. Those opposed to such payoffs feel powerless to do anything about them; the bureaucracy of government is too large, and the officials involved too powerful. The patrons of the Golf Hotel might well be deeply involved in such schemes. If your uncle Gustav was also involved, then you must do something to counter it. Unless . . . unless Gustav was playing a double game.

After hanging up your clothes, you stretch out on your bed and ponder what might be going on. Your first day in Corvarra has certainly been eventful. You wonder who will approach you next.

Your thoughts are interrupted by the sound of a helicopter returning to the valley floor. The memory of the avalanche and your escape from the White Death floods back.

There is a knock at the door. You freeze. What now?

"Room service. I have a package for you," a voice announces. There is no accent; the English is flat and unidentifiable.

"Just leave it outside the door," you reply on the spur of the moment.

"Certainly. You will enjoy this present," says the voice.

Turn to page 95.

The wind howls for several hours, and you think you can hear the rumbling roar of avalanches high on the mountain slopes. Sleep is impossible. Toward morning you hear voices downstairs. They are not distinct, but the words are sometimes sharp and argumentative. You must find out what is up.

Slowly and carefully you edge your way to the stairs and creep down, one step at a time. In the main room by the fireplace sit Chin Lee and Dominique with the white-haired man, who has remained anonymous. Surprisingly, he seems to be in control of the discussion. You listen in.

White Hair: "We must confront the issue immediately. Let us not delay. Either we get cooperation, or we move to another plan and forget this amiable but apparently useless relative of our dear old friend Gustav."

Dominique: "Fair enough, but we have time. The payment is not due until the fourth of next month. Why are you so impatient?"

Chin Lee: "You do not understand the seriousness of the event, do you, my dear Dominique? Dear Gustav set in motion a plan to disrupt the financial markets of Germany, France, Italy, and England. It is in place, it is running, and we hold the final key. Everything we have banked on, planned for, the control of banks, stock markets, and even governments, depends on us using that money in those accounts. Someone is draining them. We must put a stop to it."

Turn to page 84.

NAME:	Chin Lee
AGE:	54
ALIAS:	Forgotten Foot
BIRTHPLACE:	China
HOME:	Hong Kong; aboard a Chinese junk registered in Panama
OCCUPATION:	illegal operations: smuggling guns, drugs, and people; counterfeit art objects and jewelry
DESCRIPTION:	5'4", 162 lb, black hair, black eyes, walks with a slight limp

MISC: Chin Lee is the son of Chinese warlord Hun Lee, from the Mongolian Plateau. Hun Lee was famous for spiking his victims' heads on short poles, which he then drove into the ground surrounding the towns that he captured. By one count alone, Hun Lee spiked more than 16,000 heads in a three-year period. In early 1947, he deposited vast wealth into an account in Hong Kong. Immediately thereafter, Hun Lee died, cause unknown.

Chin Lee developed a taste for gambling in Hong Kong; he is reported to have lost his entire fortune, which at one time amounted to more than 250 million U.S. dollars.

Go on to the next page.

Chin Lee has been rumored to be involved with slavery. Vietnamese boat people and escapees from mainland China have been kidnapped by Chin Lee's men and sold to wealthy clients as household servants or workers in factories that produce counterfeit art objects, jewelry, and automatic weapons.

International bank audits show that Chin Lee and Gustav Hendrikson had joint accounts in a Bahamian bank. Also, connections in Thailand with opium lords are suspected.

When you have finished reading all the reports, remember to turn to page 36.

"Come in, come in! Soup's on! Tea's hot! Fire's warm! Come in at once!" Muscles commands from the doorway of the hut. Dominique gives you a look; Arte whistles one of his tunes; and Chin Lee shuffles inside. Your eye rests on the spot where the rifle was moments before; now there is a knapsack resting there. The rifle is nowhere to be seen.

If you decide to go with Dominique, turn to page 60.

If you decide to vamoose, turn to page 81.

If you decide to meet with Arte, turn to page 99.

NAME:	Arnold Morris
AGE:	38
ALIAS:	Arte Funk
BIRTHPLACE:	Iowa, U.S.A.
HOME:	Los Angeles, CA
OCCUPATION:	musician
DESCRIPTION:	5'7", 175 lb, long, dirty-blond hair, flabby

MISC: Arte Funk is an American rock star whose band, The Dimwits, is a mixture of folk, rap, punk, heavy metal, and grunge. Arte wears oversize farmer coveralls, a hard hat, and a chain metal vest. Members of his band wear monks' robes in dark red. The Dimwits have remained at the top of the charts for the past 18 months, but Arte is believed to have quit the band. (Band could be a cover-up for international underworld activities.)

Arte grew up in a small town in Iowa, where he never finished high school. He has a long rap sheet with the police in Iowa and California. (Possible blackmail opportunity.)

Arte's latest reported passion is snowboarding.

Go on to the next page.

Arte has avoided the press for the past year after a bad incident with the police on drug charges. Travels in tough circles. Always needs money. Name mentioned in connection with bribery attempts on elected officials in the U.S.—no conviction.

When you have finished reading all the reports, remember to turn to page 36.

As you stand there in the arena of death, the snow lessens, the wind drops, and the clouds scatter. There is silence as the earth returns to the calmness of the morning. The smell of cordite fills the air and is the only reminder that the body lying on the snow is a real corpse and not a pretend dead man.

"What do you want?" you ask Dominique.

"You know exactly what I want."

"What do you mean?" you reply, playing for time.

"The number to the remaining accounts in the Bahamas bank and the last Swiss account. Don't play dumb with me."

"I don't have any numbers," you say angrily. Your patience is wearing thin. These people are willing to kill for their greed. Anger floods you and turns to action. You throw yourself at Dominique, catching her off guard and slamming her to the ground. You grasp the Beretta and fling it with all your might into the snowy distance.

"That will be enough of that," Chin Lee says, standing lightly on his skis. "You will tell us the numbers in good time. I am more patient than the others. But my patience does have its downside. There can be pain involved. We shall see. For now, we will return to the mountain hut. Dominique, you lead the way. First, however, let us rid ourselves of this baggage."

Turn to page 104.

NAME:	Dominique Pascal
AGE:	17
ALIAS:	None
BIRTHPLACE:	Bangkok, Thailand
HOME:	Paris, France; Chang Mai, Thailand
OCCUPATION:	student
DESCRIPTION:	5'6", 120 lb, black hair, blue-green eyes, athletic

MISC: Dominique Pascal, a French citizen born and brought up in Bangkok, is the daughter of French rubber plantation owners who escaped Vietnam after the French military disaster at Dien Bien Phu in 1954. Her father, Albert, has long been suspected of smuggling and is on Interpol's list of wanted characters. He was last seen in the northern part of Thailand in the border town of Chang Mai. He has been reported killed in a firefight in the jungle with an outlaw guerrilla group—no confirmation; believed to be connected to international underworld group.

Pascal has been in school in France for the last three years. She has developed a love of skiing and is often found in the Dolomites on vacation. She has no apparent connection with the business of her father, but the source of her generous income is open for debate.

Go on to the next page.

Pascal speaks Thai, mandarin Chinese, English, and French. She has studied ballet and traditional Thai dance forms.

Pascal could be a very valuable contact. Updated report is advised.

When you have finished reading all the reports, remember to turn to page 36.

32

You survey the snow and clouds outside. It is a serious storm, but then, mountain storms can leave as quickly as they arrive. You weigh the options: leave now or wait out the storm. After all, who is this Arte Funk? Why believe him? Maybe you should ask him more about himself.

*If you push Funk for more details,
turn to page 82.*

*If you decide to follow his advice and leave
immediately, turn to page 74.*

*If you decide to wait out the storm,
turn to page 71.*

Three months later your body washes up on a beach on the island of Capri. Little notice is taken of the event. The world is more concerned with the collapse of several governments, the explosion of vicious wars in Africa and Latin America, and the formation of an alliance between Japan and China. An international business group has gained control of the world's major money markets. It is headed by a woman named Isabella Hendrikson.

The End

34

You're nervous but excited about the picnic. It could be the ideal way to get to know these people and find out what's on their minds. They might very well be the people you are after.

That afternoon and night pass uneventfully. At 7:30 sharp the next morning you join the group, ready for the ski picnic.

"Welcome! So glad you are joining us. We will all feel safer having so distinguished a skier as you in our midst," says a corpulent Asian gentleman you take to be Chin Lee.

"Really, I'm nothing important in the ski world," you reply modestly, but secretly you are pleased at being so addressed. Actually, despite your rather young years, you are regarded by some as a potential world ski racing champion. Your downhill results in the U.S. have been impressive in the Junior Nationals and recently in the Nationals. You have been invited to two summer racing camps, one at Mt. Hood, Oregon, and the other in Las Lenas, Argentina. These are selection camps for the U.S. Ski Team.

Turn to page 48.

So now you have read the confidential reports prepared by the Soboldt Agency, Ltd. of London, England, for your aunt. But many questions remain: Why choose you to do the search? Why not continue with Soboldt? What are the comments about possible blackmail subjects and secret files on Hendrikson all about? Who are the Soboldt people? Is there something fishy about the whole setup? Are you being set up, and if so, why? What do they want from you?

Different possibilities hit you: First off, you could be being used as some kind of shield. But for whom, and why? Also, Uncle Gustav left a will in which you are named as the sole heir to his fortune, if indeed there is any left. Maybe someone wants you out of the way. Maybe, just maybe, the whole thing is a scam run by some government to smoke out some high-placed crooks in Europe. Maybe all these people are secret agents, and you are a guinea pig.

Money needed to fuel the expanding economies of both developed and developing nations has posed a worldwide problem. Fortunes are being made by businessmen, government officials, lawyers, and bankers at the expense of the people. It's like a free-for-all. The rewards are so great that the risks seem minimal.

Turn to page 19.

Suddenly your instinct takes over, and you regard the package with new suspicion. Perhaps this is a bomb, you think. I'll get rid of it, you tell yourself. A good snowbank will be the place. It will absorb any blast, and I'll inform the local police. The snow should keep it from hurting any innocent bystander.

You creep out into the hallway and down the stairs, avoiding the elevator. No sense in attracting attention. You gain the outside unobserved. A huge bank of snow, left over from the winter's plowing, borders the parking lot of the hotel. It doesn't take you long to bury the package deeply, and, you hope, safely.

You make your way to the police station. There you are subjected to detailed questioning before a team is sent out to examine the bomb. Hours later the team returns; the item is just what it appeared to be, a basket of fruit. You are warned not to harass the police. They are angry, to say the least. For your part, you are embarrassed, but you vow to yourself to remain on guard.

Turn to page 5.

38

Suddenly a sharp stinging assaults your eyes. Snow and sleet are falling heavily. A huge cloud descends and obscures the track and the welcoming woods below. Frantically you swipe at your eyes, but still you cannot see. You feel as if you are inside a pillow of goose down. Your skis founder in the thick new snow that has blanketed the track. You are stopped dead.

In a whiteout like this there is no telling up from down. You are completely disoriented, and any movement on your skis suddenly gives you a dizzy feeling, a vertigo. There is nothing to do but stop . . . at least for the time being.

The blizzard plays around the mountain peaks, and the snow piles up below. Your energy ebbs as your body tries its best to keep warm at the core. When your core temperature —the temperature in your chest cavity—drops below eighty-five degrees, it will not go back up regardless of what you do.

Turn to page 98.

"You are also staying at the Golf, no doubt?" Siegfried says.

You nod.

Siegfried glances at his watch. "It's already ten, and I haven't eaten a thing. I hate to miss a meal—why don't you join me for a late breakfast? You must be starved, particularly after such a near miss."

Didn't he just finish gobbling down that panino? you think to yourself. Nevertheless, this could be an excellent opportunity to do some initial spadework and find out what is going on in the Golf Hotel. Siegfried seems to be the type of person who would know all the juice—a born snooper. You have not studied the files yet. You were planning to do that this evening after surveying the guests in the hotel. A false step now could be unfortunate, if not dangerous. Remember, these people play for keeps.

You could refuse his invitation to breakfast and suggest a meeting later, giving you time to go to your room and study the files. Or you could accept and begin your investigation immediately. Siegfried looks useful.

If you decide to refuse the invitation and return to your room, turn to page 15.

If you decide to accept the late breakfast invitation with Siegfried, turn to page 16.

40

Tons of snow cascade down the steep slope. You can't outrun it—your only hope is to ski out of its way, off to the side. Once again the air fills with snow crystals, making it hard to breathe.

Cranking a turn to your right, you squirt out of the avalanche's path and hug a cliff face. Your skis slam against the rock. The avalanche roars on toward the bottom, leaving you unharmed. A thought runs through your head: *The sharp cracking sound could have been a shot fired at you, and instead of hitting you, it caused the avalanche.*

I'm getting paranoid, you think. On the other hand, it is essential to stay alert at all times.

The avalanche has left a path of junky snow. You edge out carefully and, after checking your skis, head down. There is still powder on the sides of the slope, but soon it runs out. The lower part of the mountain is a hard-packed, icy piste. Finally you reach the bottom where the slopes converge into one open slope for beginners. There are very few skiers at this time of year, but the little kiosk that sells hot coffee, soda, small sandwiches called panini, and chocolate is open.

Standing next to the kiosk is a short, rotund man wearing a bright yellow tweed suit with vivid green checks. His handlebar mustache curls upward, partially covering his cheeks. He is munching on a panino and holding a paper cup of steaming coffee.

Turn to page 12.

SOBOLDT AGENCY
London
CURRENT CONFIDENTIAL REPORT
NOT FOR CLIENT USE

**This is an in-house evaluation of
the subject GUSTAV HENDRIKSON
and not to be disseminated to client.
For use as information
only to our files.**

HENDRIKSON, GUSTAV

Subject Gustav Hendrikson has been under surveillance by Interpol, the Japanese intelligence group, and the Thai secret service since 10/87.

Reference to this man has been found in financial journals in Europe and Asia. He seems to have been involved in international financial dealings between governments and corporations. Some links to oil-producing countries have also been found.

Name Gustav Hendrikson is an alias: real name seems to be Anthony Squibb. Born in northern Wales and educated in Germany and Sweden. Father minor diplomat, mother Danish, a novelist but not well known.

Go on to the next page.

Wife seems to be unaware of his origins, believing him to be what he says he is: an investor specializing in Asian companies. Hendrikson/Squibb has had bank accounts in Liechtenstein, Switzerland, and the Maldive Islands. Figures unknown due to bank regulations for secrecy, but amounts believed to be, by reliable estimates, in the 20–30 million dollar U.S. category.

Sole heir to his estate is the child of his deceased sister. FOLLOW UP ON THIS HEIR.

Turn to page 8.

Amsterdam police have been unsuccessful in finding or identifying the car involved in this hit-and-run accident. Reports of a similar type car were made by the German police regarding high-speed chase on autobahn to Munich the night of the accident. Police unable to catch car. Note: Autobahns do not have speed limit for far left lane. Unusual for police to chase cars unless they have some special information or reason.

SECOND EVENT

On the same day in Rome, Italy, Inga Maidorf was found with her throat slit in a street behind the Vatican. Her passport identified her as a naturalized U.S. citizen of 20 years of age. Her U.S. address was 153 Canal Street, New York, NY.

The U.S. Embassy has failed to find any relative to claim the body. Her remains were frozen and stored pending results of relative search by the U.S. government.

Go on to the next page.

In her handbag was a receipt for the deposit of 6 million dollars U.S. in a Liechtenstein bank. No account number, of course, was given, but the bank was the same bank as two of the accounts apparently used by Hendrikson. Also, a confirmation slip for a hotel in Corvarra, Italy was found. The Hotel named was the Golf Hotel and the reservation was for late April.

MISC: seen with REGINALD DUNBARTON. Dunbarton is a disbarred lawyer from London who has been known to deal with organized crime figures.

When you have finished reading all the reports, remember to turn to page 36.

"Okay, here we are," the driver announces in a heavy English accent. "The track is over there. Beware of the narrow valley. Avalanches can happen. I will meet you back here at dusk. Have a good tour." With a wave and a smile, he departs. You look at the departing Unimog, wondering if you will ever see it again.

The sun climbs into the sky. The snow on the flanks of the great mountains will begin to work loose from the rock faces by late morning. Already small showers of ice, snow, and rock cascade down with rattling sounds.

While you check your equipment, Dominique leans over and whispers to you. She is careful not to attract the attention of the others. You remember the report on her: student, lives in Paris and Thailand, speaks mandarin Chinese. You remind yourself to check the files once again. Valuable clues could be found there, clues that might save your life.

"Meet me down the trail from the hut that we'll stop at for our lunch. Don't tell anyone. Your life is in danger." She moves away on her cross-country skis.

You wait for Chin Lee to approach you with the same proposition. Things often happen in threes. But as this thought enters your head, you remind yourself that there have been only 2 deaths. So far.

Turn to page 86.

48

The group listens to you and waits for Chin Lee's reply.

"I like modesty in the young," Chin Lee says. "Your exploits on the race course have been noted in the European press. Here, let me introduce Monsieur Arte Funk, the well-known American singer, and also Mademoiselle Dominique Pascal." There is a third person, young, male, silent. He bulges with pectoral muscles through his turtleneck. Not even the hint of a smile crosses the taut skin of his face. No one bothers to introduce him.

"So, now let us partake of these mountains so beautiful," Chin Lee says with an oily tone and a gesture of warmth and kindness. But the eyes in his smiling face are cold and reptilian. They survey you.

"Fine, I'm ready," you reply. "Where to?"

"Oh, do not be impatient. We have wonderful things in store."

The woman named Dominique whispers to Muscles, and he runs off on some errand. Skis and packs are loaded into a Unimog—a four-wheel-drive Mercedes Benz mountain vehicle—and the driver insists that all climb into the cab. Moments later you are chugging along a mountain road that is half snow, half mud, headed for the back country.

You notice a cloud front moving in slowly from the south and wonder if the day will be short. Mountain storms can be vicious.

Turn to page 57.

Breakfast, you soon discover, is far from what Siegfried has in mind. He takes you to a small inn near the hotel, on a back street crowded with shops and a few mean-looking bars.

"Here, we will take coffee here," Siegfried says, but you see no restaurant. The place he indicates is a shabby bar. You enter through the door into a smoke-filled room with half a dozen men in overalls, boots, and rough sweaters huddled over coffee and little glasses of amber-colored liquid, which you take for brandy. *Ugh*, you think to yourself. *How could anyone take a drink so early in the day?*"

Siegfried nods at the man behind the bar, who in turn beckons to another man who rises from his chair and locks the door. The slatted blinds are pulled, and the rest of the men in the room turn toward you.

Turn to page 56.

50

You sink into a large, overstuffed armchair in the lobby and pick up a copy of the *Herald Tribune*. Opening the paper, you cover your face with it. Whoever these people are, you hope they will leave you alone until you can get out of this town and head back to the good old U.S. of A.

As you are sitting there, your eyes happen to glance over the headlines of the paper. One article sticks out:

PATTERN OF BRIBERY AND CORRUPTION
SEEN AT HIGHEST LEVELS

Bonn, Germany. AP. High-ranking agents of Interpol, the international law enforcement information-sharing agency, reported today a break in their investigation of bribery and corruption at the highest levels of government and business in some of the world's leading countries, including Japan, Italy, France, Germany, and the U.S.

Interpol has uncovered a plot to use an enormous pool of funds (said to be more than 800 million U.S. dollars) to buy off politicians and major world figures in a massive attempt to control world monetary markets.

The break came when agents discovered the involvement of a wealthy international consultant. The man, Gustav Hendrikson, died in a suspicious automobile accident in Amsterdam, Holland, several weeks ago.

Turn to page 87.

52

An ax leans against the wall of the hut, and a rifle rests on a crude chair underneath the overhang of the roof. You like neither one. You wonder what is in store for you now.

In the doorway stands Muscles. This time there is a trace of a smile on his face. He holds out a cup of steaming brew, available for the first taker.

"Psst! Psst!" comes a hiss from Dominique. "Come with me," she whispers, moving up to your side. You nod. You feel like a pinball being knocked around in some giant electronic game: no matter where you turn, there is someone who wants something from you.

Arte nudges you almost at the same time and gives a meaningful wink. A whiff of garlic accompanies the wink. Dominique darts an anxious look. She is impatient.

Muscles is now joined by a wiry, white-skinned, white-haired individual, who shouts a greeting that seems more like a command. His English has overtones of an Oxford accent.

"Welcome to paradise in the mountains. Above you is the abode of the gods. Joining the gods will be their handmaidens, a storm that brings with it snow, rain, hail, and a reminder of our frailty. Be prepared for a long stay here. There is no going back today—maybe not even tomorrow." He smiles and vanishes into the darkness of the mountain hut.

Turn to page 92.

That was last week. You accepted, not knowing quite what you were getting into. Isabella airmailed you a computer disc with all the information she had on the suspects and the business that Uncle Gustav was involved with. Also enclosed was a note:

> Read this, study it, and then destroy it. Here are money, credit cards, and train and hotel reservations. I have included the telephone number of a friend in Rome who could be of help—use it only in an emergency. Memorize it, then destroy it. Good luck, be careful, and remember the honor of our family rests on your shoulders.

Two turns, tight and perfect; then a long, slow arc in the deeper powder near a protruding rock face. Your skis hang beautifully, your upper body almost motionless, your legs absorbing the terrain and pushing the skis ever so slightly into the arcing turns.

CRACK!

A sharp noise blasts through the still air. Adrenaline floods your body. Was that the sound of an avalanche or of a shot?

Avalanche!

Turn to page 40.

54

Finally you reach the sanctuary of your room at the Golf Hotel. The room is small, but from the windows, and especially from your private terrace, you have a magnificent view of the Dolomites, those proud pinnacles that guard the Alps. The snowfields sparkle in the late morning light.

Your laptop computer sits on the desk next to the bed. *Wait a minute. Has someone moved it? Has someone used it?* you wonder. There is some subtle change, but it could have been the maid. The battery light is blinking, indicating the computer is at the ebb of its power. No problem. You plug it in. *But hold it. You didn't leave it on, did you?* you ask yourself. You're not sure.

Turn to page 18.

56

"So, now we are together. We are all friends, and you are safe—at least for the time being," Siegfried announces. His attitude is firm, and he is definitely in control. This ridiculous little man has turned into a very firm commander in the twinkling of an eye. You hear it in his voice, see it in his eyes, and his manner is no longer bumptious.

"There is a decision you must make, my young friend, and no one can help you make it," Siegfried says. "Certainly, we can hold you here or take you away to Rome or Paris or Helsinki or anywhere we wish. But—and this is a big but —we would prefer that you avoid any and all unpleasantness and freely join with us. We need you much more than your aunt, however gracious she may be."

"My aunt—what has she got to do with all this? And why me? I mean, it seems that everyone needs good old me. I know nothing. I don't even know what this is all about. Somebody murdered my uncle and stole his money. Is it Uncle Gustav's will you are after?"

"Not quite, but you are getting closer. The will —no. But the power the will gives extends to much more than the money. Do you understand?" Siegfried says.

The man guarding the door suddenly hisses. He holds his hand up. "Something's happening out there," he says.

"What?" Siegfried asks.

Turn to page 107.

Chin Lee chatters along, barely understandable. Arte Funk zeroes in on you. His accent is country-and-western, and his breath smells as if he works in a garlic factory. His bug eyes seem to suggest poor health and a bad diet. You wonder if he is trying to copy the last days of Elvis Presley.

"Now lissen here, pardner. I'm gonna be your friend, your real good and true friend. And you gonna need one, I'm tellin' the truth," he says amid clouds of garlic fumes. You fight to keep from moving back from him.

"Great, Mr. Funk. Everyone needs friends," you muster.

"None of this 'Mr.' stuff. Arte, Arte's my handle. Now lissen to me. When we get to the hut where we break for grub, you and me, we'll find some time to be alone and talk. Don't trust the others," he says in a very low voice that you can barely hear. Fortunately the roar of the engine and the babble of conversation between Chin Lee and Dominique covers up what Arte is saying.

Thirty minutes later, the Unimog draws to a stop beside a snowdrift that must have been huge in midwinter but now is a sodden, soiled lump of snow. Chin Lee leads the way from the Unimog; the skis and packs are unloaded quickly. There is something odd going on, you feel. No one really says anything that is out of the ordinary, but you get the feeling that they are all on edge.

Turn to page 47.

You can't bring yourself to leave Siegfried to the fate of the thugs, so you grab him and practically throw him into the entranceway of a dingy shop on the narrow street. And just in time. Two men rush by, and you know they are the killers.

"Stay here," you command Siegfried. "I'll check the place out, and if it's clear, I'll come back. If I don't return, you're on your own."

"You don't have to help me," Siegfried says.

"No time for discussion, we're all in this together," you reply. Then you are off down the dark hallway and into a storage room. There is little light, and you bump into a large wooden box that blocks your path.

"Drat!" you exclaim loudly.

"Who's that?" comes a voice.

You stop, frozen in your tracks. The question has been phrased in English—very strange indeed for a storage room in an Italian town.

"Is that you, Peter?" comes the voice.

You take a risk. "No, I'm not Peter."

"Then who are you?"

"I'm out of here!" is your reply. And you don't wait to find out who the person is. You make it back to Siegfried, who seems composed, almost relaxed.

Turn to page 4.

60

You decide to talk with Dominique Pascal and see what she has to say. But you delay your meeting by entering the mountain hut and accepting a cup of steaming tea from the white-haired friend of Muscles. The tea is strong and good and comforting. But the memory of the avalanche gnaws at the edge of your brain.

Reluctantly you leave the warmth of the hut, murmuring some excuse about needing to adjust the bindings on your skis. There is silence in the hut; you feel eyes turned on you, watching, waiting, staring. Then you are outside. It has begun to snow in earnest. The flakes are small and hard and sting when they hit your face. The mountains are obscured. The wind has picked up.

"Follow me," Dominique says to you. "Hurry. No, don't take skis."

She slips around several large boulders and along a cliff. It is tough going through the snow, but you follow as quickly as prudence allows. Close to twenty minutes later, you almost bump into a Sno-Cat hunkered down in the storm. The engine is ticking over nicely, and the wiper blades have created two large half-moon shapes on the windshield.

"Get in!" Dominique commands. You don't like her tone but obey nonetheless.

Turn to page 93.

You can't resist yet another run. This time there are several people on the chairlift. Two of them are close to you in age and turn out to be on the Italian Junior National ski team.

"*Prego,* would you take a run with us?" one of them, named Antonio, asks. The other doesn't speak English but smiles and points down the run you just finished.

"Sure, love to," you reply.

Whoa! What a run. The two Italians show you a line down the slope you had not noticed. It is fast, really fast. When you get to the bottom, you are whipped. Unfortunately, your new friends are leaving Corvarra to head back to Rome. You'll be on your own again.

The walk back to the Golf is short, and you feel good and tired. The thought of your uncle's death and the people who might be connected with it seems remote and unreal. You can deal with all that tomorrow, you think.

You walk through the hotel lobby and up to your room. As you search your pockets for the key, you are surprised to find your mysterious gift still waiting for you in the hallway—a large basket of fruit and candies with a bright red bow.

"Hey, why not?" you say. "I'm hungry. A nice piece of fruit and some chocolate will do me good right now."

Turn to page 112.

62

"You will have to trust me," Siegfried tells you as you take your seats in the back of the small café. "My name is Pierro Francesco. My name is not Siegfried von Holtzgraf. I am not Hungarian, or Austrian, or Russian. I am an Italian investigator for a secret commission. We are tracking down an organization of very powerful international criminals. Their bag of tricks includes murder along with bribery and blackmail."

"Great! But why me? I don't know anything about all this," you say.

"Ah, but you do not know whether you know it or not. Your uncle Gustav Hendrikson was one of us. It was he who risked his life as an undercover agent, penetrating deep into their highest circles."

"What circles?" you ask.

"There is a group called the Meridians. They represent a select number of wealthy individuals around the world. This group has been in existence for more than one hundred years. New members are carefully selected and trained to replace the aged or dead ones. They try to control the world through financial markets, government, and the military. Often they succeed."

"Okay, okay. But who's my uncle to you?" you ask.

Turn to page 70.

64

Moments later you drop off the edge and cut sharp, short turns down the steep face. The new snow billows in front of you and makes the turns a delight. Down you go, matching Gerard turn for turn. Your legs burn, your breath becomes short, but your heart soars with the excitement of the run. Mountains have always been your friends.

Finally you are at the bottom of the couloir. It terminates in a jumble of rocks, small bushes, and trees. You are on the opposite side of the mountain from the Golf Hotel and the mountain hut. Perhaps now you are safe.

"I'll get you to the train for Rome, then you are on your own," Gerard says.

"What is this all about?" you ask.

"Money, power, greed—simple and as old as life itself," Gerard replies.

Turn to page 13.

"Who are they?" you gasp, choking on the smoke.

"If you think they will be your friends, think again. This is not a police force. This, my stupid young friend, is the opposition. We are like babes in the woods compared to them. Here, take this weapon. Use it if you wish. You're on your own now," Chin Lee says.

You stare at the flat black automatic, drop it to the floor, and head for the door.

You never make it. An explosion rocks the mountain hut, and the final moments of your life are an intricate web of flying, fragmented memories.

The End

It's your aunt! She is standing in front of you with a sweet and innocent smile on her face. Beside her is a middle-aged man in tweeds smoking a cigar and smiling. He has a briefcase with him.

"It's all over. I was wrong. So, I hope you had some nice skiing and some good meals in this lovely hotel. Mr. Dunbarton here is an old family friend and lawyer. He and your uncle went to university together. Didn't you, Reggie?" Your aunt looks mildly befuddled, but your instincts are on high alert.

Outside the hotel, klaxons of police cars upset the tranquility of the mountain town. You know where they are headed, and the thought of Siegfried being gunned down is revolting to you. I've got to get away from these people, you think to yourself. Immediately!

"Reggie has been so kind as to arrange a car to take us back to Rome, and then you and I can fly back home," says your aunt. "Oh, he does have some papers for you to sign. Why don't we go up and pack your things? We have to be getting on our way."

"Great. But just a minute, I need to get some things I left in the hotel checkroom. I'll be just a minute. I'm glad things have turned out well," you say, moving off rapidly.

Turn to page 114.

68

"Don't!" Siegfried screams out as you leap from your chair and make for the café door.

You run right into the arms of a stocky Asian man, who executes two classic karate movements and renders you helpless.

"We have been looking for you," he says. "Do be helpful and come quietly."

"Chin Lee," Siegfried says calmly, almost in disbelief. The last you see of Siegfried is a figure desperately trying to escape, only to be stopped by one of Chin Lee's men.

The End

At the top of the mountain a cluster of signs points to the different towns of the Sella Ronda. You choose the piste that drops into the town of Arabba. Hurriedly you put on your boots, zip your parka, snap on your skis, and with one last search of the small crowd, push off.

The snow is really good, and your skis find their way down a steep pitch that causes your blood to pulse with pure love of mountains and life. For the time being you are free of the madness back at the Golf Hotel.

In front of you two skiers have stopped and are watching you. A shiver of fear and premonition overtakes you. Could these be more of the devils? you ask yourself. The piste drops straight toward them, but there is an alternative: a headwall or cliff that drops away to the right. Several ski tracks lead to the lip. Someone must have skied it.

You don't hesitate but carve a beautiful high-speed arcing turn and head for the lip. Before you know it, you are over the lip, catching huge air, and then down into superb powder snow up to your knees. You follow two tracks that plunge to the valley floor and the town of Arabba.

Turn to page 75.

"Simply put, the Meridians have built up an eight-hundred-million-dollar war chest to bribe some very powerful people in Europe, Asia, and the U.S. If they succeed, they will control and dominate the monetary systems of the world. Then we will all be peasants working for them. Your uncle had begun to empty some of the secret accounts of the money. He also made a list of the people to be bribed or who had already been bribed."

"That's why he was killed, wasn't it?" you say.

"Yes, as was the poor young lady, Inga Maidorf. She was one of our agents. Her fiancé is working undercover as a ski instructor and guide. His name is Gerard."

"You still haven't answered my question. Why me?" you ask again.

"Simple. Your uncle named you in his will as his sole heir. You alone have access to his papers and his safe-deposit box. We believe the names and account numbers are there. They too believe that. That is why they want you—alive, I might add."

"But my aunt Isabella?" you say.

"She is one of them. Your uncle found that out all too late in the game," he says, lighting up a foul-smelling cigarette. He sips his coffee thoughtfully.

"So, what now?" you ask. A rush of fear overwhelms you.

Turn to page 116.

The wind increases in intensity, tucking drifts of snow around the mountain hut. You expect the worst from this group of people, but you maintain your calm over a simple meal of hot soup, pungent cheese, and thick, coarse peasant salami. The conversation at dinner and afterward turns to world politics, the energy crisis, and endangered species. Chin Lee speaks passionately about world population as the greatest threat of all. His agile mind reels off the population of many countries: "India, 675 million people; China, 1.2 billion; Western Europe, 275 million; the U.S. at 260 million. Growing, growing, growing, out of control."

Finally the evening draws to a close. The fire in the huge stone fireplace is banked, one light is left on, and you are all about to retire to bunk rooms. By now, you feel almost relaxed. Your fears recede only to come rushing back when Muscles says, "I warn everyone, do not leave alone. Only go as a party. This storm is worse than I expected."

The words seem to hide a deeper meaning, implying that you are a prisoner. Reluctantly, you leave the relative comfort of the fireplace and carefully climb the worn wooden stairs to one of the small rooms.

Turn to page 21.

The snow intensifies, and the wind builds drifts. The track becomes worse than before. You build a small shelter from boughs and hunker down out of the wind. An hour passes; you are very cold. You try to think of warm things, but it does no good.

"I've got to skedaddle," you say out loud. Your words are lost in the wind. Finally you get back on your skis, and trusting your instinct, you set off in what you hope is the direction of the town.

As if by miracle, the wind drops, the snow ceases, and there below, you see the town within your grasp. There seems to be no one behind you—at least for now. You push ahead as fast as you can go.

Who are these people? What do they want? What did Uncle Gustav really do? are the thoughts that assault you as you work your way back to town. "I'll find out, if it kills me," you say. "I'll meet with that Siegfried guy; he might be the key to the whole thing."

The day after your safe return, you arrange to meet with Siegfried. He insists on meeting for a late breakfast.

What's up with this guy and his thing about late breakfasts? you wonder.

Turn to page 49.

74

You leave the mountain hut, not sure what faces you, but you feel you must make a move somehow.

The storm is backing off, and the clouds are breaking just enough to reveal the mountains. The path you follow is clogged with new snow, but you push through it with strength built up over hours of training and conditioning. Within twenty minutes, you manage to reach the spot Arte described as being almost an hour away.

Near a vertical rock face is Muscles, whose real name is Gerard, with a pack and climbing ropes. He also holds two pairs of short, wide alpine skis, made for the backcountry.

"Hurry, we will climb this face. Do not worry, I have already placed pitons in the rock. It is less dangerous than it looks. We haven't much time."

Fortunately, you have ski mountaineering boots on, and their Vibram lug soles are perfect for the rock climb ahead. They will double as ski boots as well.

The climb is short and steep, and despite the assurances of Gerard, the pitons driven into the firm rock, and the ropes, the ascent is scary. At last you crest the cliff and find a flat, firm spot. Below is a very steep gully filled with snow. It drops straight down and seems to vanish. You feel a rush of excitement tinged with fear.

"Put on the skis. Follow me," Gerard says.

Turn to page 64.

The run to the bottom turns from steep to gentle, and the slushy snow on the bottom half of the mountain makes skiing tricky. But you reach the town safely. It doesn't take long to hire a car to take you to the town of Trento and from there straight on to Rome. The next morning you present yourself at the U.S. embassy and demand to talk with the ambassador. You of course are turned over to a young, minor official who sees you as yet another obnoxious tourist in trouble.

Your story sounds unbelievable—even to you—and the embassy assistant rolls her eyes in disbelief. But finally she says, "I'm turning you over to one of our special people. Good luck."

The special person turns out to be connected to an intelligence group concentrating on crime at high levels of government and industry throughout the world. This person takes everything you say seriously, particularly when you identify yourself as a relative of Gustav Hendrikson.

The next forty-eight hours are a blur as you are shuttled to Paris, then Bonn, and finally to Washington, D.C. Papers recovered from a safe-deposit vault in Brussels, Belgium, provide a complete list of government officials from around the world, who have either been bribed or are ready to accept bribes.

Turn to page 103.

76

Then Arte's voice drops to little more than a whisper, and he says in a voice devoid of any accent, "Get out while you can. Your life is in greater danger than you will ever believe. That avalanche was no accident."

"Who are you?" you ask excitedly. "I mean, what do you have to do with these people?"

"Let's just say that I'm a friend—a friend that you need right now. Leave it at that. I'll cover your retreat, but you make tracks, and make tracks fast. Don't go back the way we came. Here, I've drawn a map for you. Go to the right of the hut when you leave the door. Then after about a hundred meters, take a sharp left and head uphill until you get to a flat piece of terrain. It should take you about an hour. Wait there."

"It's snowing," you reply.

"Well, we can't manage everything. Do the best you can. I'm afraid that if you wait until the storm is over, it might be too late."

Turn to page 32.

78

You leave Siegfried and run for it. After all, who is he to you? You don't know him. Maybe it's no coincidence that every time he's been around you've had a brush with death. It's time for a break.

"Run, feet, run!" you exclaim, accelerating around the corner and heading for the safety of the lobby of the Golf Hotel.

Blam! Blam! Blam!

Three sharp explosions reverberate through the narrow street. You know they are shots, and you envisage the crumpled body of Siegfried leaking blood onto the cold cobblestones of the street. The thought enters your brain that the next shots will be aimed at you!

You summon all the energy and willpower needed to make this the fastest sprint of your life. Your lungs supply oxygen to the blood, your muscles respond with amazing dedication, and you seem to have almost a heightened sense of time and space and vision.

Turn to page 83.

GUSTAV HENDRIKSON & ASSOCIATES, LTD.

Limited information on this group. Government files in London and in Paris, where there are branches of his organization, are marked CLOSED or have been removed.

Initial investigation indicates that this is a shield for some other type of group, perhaps an illegal operation. Initial description says it is a group set up for foreign investment, especially in third world countries in the Pacific Rim. But there are no real supporting data.

There seems to be substantial money moving in and out of this shell of a business. Source and destination are unknown.

Swiss banking authorities report that there has been a mysterious loss of funds in two of the accounts in that country. They are as mystified as we are as to how the funds were transferred. The funds were in Hendrikson's name in a confidential but not numbered account. Total missing from the Swiss banks: 18 million U.S.

Similar report from Liechtenstein banks: amount missing: 7 million U.S.

When you have finished reading all the reports, remember to turn to page 36.

Yikes! I'm out of here, you think to yourself. I don't mind storms, and I can handle most race-courses, but I'm drawing the line at kooks and killers.

You push off with powerful strokes on your long cross-country poles. Your skis respond, and you hurtle down the track. You expect the singing crack of a high-powered rifle at any minute and the sting of a bullet in your back.

The track is straight for the first quarter of a mile, but then it dips to the right, follows a narrow line between huge boulders, and skirts the rim of a ravine. A mistake here could be disastrous. But your downhill racing experience serves you well, and the narrow cross-country skis do not falter. You are out of the rock garden and beyond the ravine in record time.

Below you lies the beginning of the heavily wooded slopes with their giant fir trees. You seek the cover of these forests, because you never know who might be after you.

Turn to page 38.

"Not good enough, Arte," you tell him. "I want to know exactly who you are. You're obviously more than just the simple rock star you pretend to be. So, 'fess up."

"I can only tell you that I represent your best interest. I'm what you would call—"

He is interrupted by the presence of Dominique Pascal in the doorway leading to the outside and Chin Lee in the doorway leading to the hut.

"Why don't both of you join us by the fire? We miss your presence," Chin Lee says in a pleasant voice. "I'm sure the skis can wait till morning. We are forced by conditions to spend the night."

Turn to page 71.

You make it to the hotel, but where to go now? Your room is probably not safe. The lobby has people in it, but would they be any protection if the killers were to burst in?

Just at that moment you hear the concierge of the hotel announce the imminent departure of the shuttle to the tramway station. There you could take a cable car to the top of the mountain and the snowfields. A group of about ten people stands outside at the shuttle stop. You must make a decision quickly.

If you decide to stay in the lobby, hoping you won't meet any killers, turn to page 50.

If you decide to hop on the shuttle, turn to page 88.

White Hair: "Enough of this. If we are not successful in getting this young American skier to join us, we must take other steps and use other means of disrupting the West. Wake that pest and get on with it. Gustav made a huge mistake in leaving everything to this young relative. If Gustav were here now, I'd kill him."

There is hesitation on the part of Chin Lee and Pascal. You feel a touch on your shoulder, and looking around, you see Muscles. He points at the group below and puts his index finger to his lips. Then he nods his head in the direction of upstairs.

You follow him; you have no other choice. He leads you quietly down the long corridor to a door in the back of the building. Carefully he lifts the heavy wooden slide bolt and pushes the door open. It leads onto a small covered porch with stairs to the woodshed below. Standing there is Arte Funk. He holds your ski clothes and equipment in his hands.

"Move, and move fast. We haven't much time," says Arte. "Gerard here will be your guide. I will stay behind to delay them. A lot depends on you, perhaps the security of the West. We will know more when we get your uncle's papers. We shall meet in Rome. Until then."

Turn to page 74.

86

You are wrong. Chin Lee does not approach you.

The group sets out on a marked track that leads deep into the mountains. Your skis are the waxless variety, and they slide easily over the firm snow. You notice that Chin Lee is surprisingly adept on skis, striding along with excellent form and energy. Double-check his report, you decide. Arte Funk, on the other hand, looks like an elephant climbing a sand dune.

The track is well-defined but very steep in sections, running through narrow valleys and across open and exposed snowfields. The altitude is sufficient to keep the snow crisp and dry despite the spring sun. But high above, walls of snow, ice, and debris begin to loosen in the warmth of the sun's rays. Tiny avalanches begin to fall well clear of the track, but clouds are moving in, and a sudden storm could change everything.

Your pace is slow, but your group covers many kilometers. The party finally arrives at a mountain hut built in the lee of a jumble of huge boulders and rocks. It is close to one o'clock. Most of the trees have been left far behind at a gentler altitude. Smoke rises from the hut in a thin thread, but it is welcoming and promises hot drink and warm food. A pair of old cross-country skis stands outside. Two sets of footprints lead into the hut, one of them quite large, the other medium sized.

Turn to page 52.

You furiously scan the paper for more news, but there is none, except for an editorial. The editorial mentions a list of people, including some very powerful and important national leaders or members of their parties or staffs, who are accepting bribes. An unidentified source reports that the list is now missing and believed to be in the hands of an unknown group who might be using it to blackmail those on the list.

"That's it!" you exclaim, forgetting where you are. Somehow that list must be connected with your uncle's will. Perhaps the will gives directions for access to the list. *No wonder they are after me*, you think. *This is a time bomb ready to explode at any minute.*

Wait a minute, you say to yourself. *Who's chasing whom? Maybe they don't even know that I might be in possession of the list. My aunt probably doesn't know anything about any of this. . . . Whoa! On the other hand, maybe she does. Maybe, just maybe, I'm being set up by her and delivered into the hands of these people. . . .*

You are interrupted in your thoughts by a familiar voice.

"There you are. I have been looking all over for you. Now I've found you. Don't worry. Everything has been taken care of. I sent you on this silly mission by mistake."

Turn to page 66.

Your skis and boots are right where you left them in the ski room near the lobby; it takes only a second to grab them and hop on the shuttle for the tram station. Your eyes survey the others on the shuttle. Looks fine, you think.

This is the last tram of the day. The snow on the high part of the mountain should be perfect, but lower down, where the sun has been shining, it will be slush. The slush will turn to ice quickly once the sun is off the slopes.

The tram rests in its station, waiting for its passengers. You move quickly and gain a position by the doorway just in case. There aren't many people, and the tram slides easily away and up to the high station above. It sways slightly and rocks as it passes over the huge towers spread out at intervals up the mountainside. The fear within you subsides ever so slightly, but you remain on guard.

Finally you reach the top station. The air is colder up here, and the wind is snuffling a bit. You move quickly and put on your skis. Corvarra is part of a ski circus or cluster of resorts that circles the Sella mountains like a chain. This group is called the Sella Ronda. From this station you can ski down the other side and end up in a different resort town, and from there you can escape this mad group of adversaries.

Turn to page 69.

NAME: Siegfried von Holtzgraf
AGE: approximately 45
ALIAS: Smootzie
BIRTHPLACE: Russia (?)
HOME: unknown
OCCUPATION: international con artist; stock schemes
DESCRIPTION: 5'5″, 165 lb, thinning gray hair, brown eyes

MISC: Suspected of bribery and murder—CONSIDER THIS MAN AN EXTREMELY DANGEROUS ADVERSARY.

Subject under surveillance for the past three years. Believed to be Russian, not Hungarian, as he has claimed in the past. The von title is believed false; he cultivates European and Asian royalty.

Subject can speak six languages: English, French, German, Serbo-Croatian, mandarin Chinese, and Russian.

Skin on fingertips of right hand appears to have been surgically removed, although subject claims to have had an accident involving an acid bath for research purposes on an art restoration project.

Could be an Interpol plant.

When you have finished reading all the reports, remember to turn to page 36.

"Okay, let's hit it!" you say, already moving for the door.

Siegfried is up and moving also; you make it to the car, jump in, and moments later are on the winding road out of town. Siegfried drives like a wild man, but he is quite competent behind the wheel.

That is until he takes a corner too high and too fast. The black sports sedan desperately tries to grip the road, but it fails. The car, with you and Siegfried inside, soars out over the cliffside and tumbles more than a thousand feet to the rocks below.

News of your accidental deaths comes as an unexpected favor to the Meridians, who proceed unchecked on their way to more domination and control.

The End

You scan the mountains and the sky. Your assessment this morning was correct: there is a storm in the mountains. Already you can feel the first drops of rain mingled with snow. The tops of the peaks are now obscured by clouds.

You look back down the track you have just come along. It is well marked but if the snow dominates the storm, the track may be lost.

You have several choices: One, you could go back now on your own. Just keep your skis on and head down. Wait for no one and make tracks. The first part is downhill, and you could be out of rifle range very quickly. Two, you could meet with Dominique. She seems sympathetic and not in the least dangerous. Perhaps she is an agent of Interpol or some other police network. Three, you could meet with old garlic breath himself.

It seems as if everyone is waiting for your next move. Even the storm hesitates, unable to decide between flurries and earnest snow or rain.

Secrets lie in the files, and more secrets still in the minds of these people, but how do you pry them out and remain healthy? And why did your aunt put you in this position? The question continues to haunt you.

Turn to page 24.

Two men sit in the warm and comfortable cab of the Cat. One of them is dressed in work clothes favored by the lift company: overalls and a light red wind jacket. He wears mountain boots and puffs on a small and unpleasantly odorous cigar. He seems to be the driver. The other man is distinguished-looking and has on, of all things, a three-piece pin-striped suit, well cut and set off by a wine-red silk tie. He holds a briefcase of fine leather in his manicured hands. Incongruously, he needs a shave.

"What's up? Who are you? How did you know we would be here?" you manage to ask in your fractured Italian with a sprinkling of German to fill in the gaps.

"We will speak English since your knowledge of Italian is as bad as your accent," the man says. Dominique chuckles at the remark. The man glares at her, and she wipes any trace of a smile from her lips.

The driver puffs on his cigar. "No time for pleasantries. We have a deal to offer you."

"I don't even know who you are," you say, amazed at your boldness in front of this frightening man.

Turn to page 110.

The lift comes to an abrupt end quite far below the summit. You push off and ski down some two or three hundred yards to another chairlift. Again there are only a few people skiing. Soon you are on the lift and headed up farther to the top. It's colder up here, and you zip your parka to the neck.

At last you reach the top station. You have a choice of several long runs to the bottom. What with the excitement of the morning and your fatigue from traveling, you decide on a wide, groomed GS run that drops and winds to the valley floor. It's a piece of cake.

The carving feeling of your skis on the snow in the wide radius takes your mind off everything but the beautiful day, the sun, the mountains, and your being a part of it.

You catch minor air off a large, rolling bump, drop into a tuck, and accelerate on the broad, gentle pitch that leads to the bottom. This is the slope used for World Cup GS races, and you feel as though you are finishing in the top five. Maybe even in first place.

The daydream is over. There are no finish gates, no cheering crowd. But it has been a great run.

Turn to page 61.

The last comment bothers you. How does the bellhop, or whoever he is, know whether or not you will enjoy this present? And what's it to him?

Just open the door, you think to yourself. *Forget the reports.* But you can't be too careful. These people play for keeps. You remember the autopsy report and the information on the girl with her throat slit in Rome.

If you ignore the gift, turn to page 109.

If you decide to open the door and accept the gift, turn to page 10.

Dominique hands you a pen she has taken from her purse. You hesitate.

"Sign it," the driver commands.

The paper must be connected with the will that your uncle wrote, leaving everything to you. But since most of his money was removed from the two Swiss accounts, you think there has to be something else these people want—perhaps some information or some piece of evidence or plan that these people are desperate for.

"Fine, I'll sign. But then what?" you ask, not wanting the answer.

"Then, my friend, maybe we will make you a partner, just like your uncle. But first, sign."

Turn to page 6.

You scan the sky for a cloud break, but it remains dense and white like a pillow, and the wind has picked up. In the thirty minutes you have been huddled here beside two rock outcroppings, snow has accumulated and wind has caused a drift of almost a foot. The track is obliterated. You're not sure how much longer you can wait before your body heat drops to dangerous levels. This storm might persist for days. You wonder what you should do.

*If you decide to wait out the storm,
turn to page 108.*

*If you decide to try and head off downhill,
turn to page 102.*

Arte Funk might be a strange dude, but your instinct tells you that he is the least committed member of the group. He could be your best bet. You wonder, however, where the two of you should meet. The mountain hut is conveniently large, with bunk rooms, a large kitchen, private quarters for the full-time summer staff, and an equipment room for climbing ropes, ice axes, and crampons.

Your question is answered by Arte Funk himself.

"Ah need some help with these skinny sticks o' mine," he says in his twang, which you think is fake. It just doesn't ring right.

"Great. I'll help, Mr. Funk," you reply, moving quickly to the equipment room.

"I tole you, ma handle is *Artee,* not this *mister* stuff. Got it?"

The two of you move off to the equipment room, which has a door to the outside as well as an access from within the hut. Arte has brought his skis inside, and they are already lying on the workbench. He moves over to them, picks up a screwdriver, and says in a loud voice, obviously for the benefit of the others in the main part of the hut, "This here ole binding is pesky as a mare with a burr."

Turn to page 76.

Dominique removes a small black Beretta from her fanny pack and points it at Gerard, holding it with both hands.

"Move, and you're dead," she says in a steely voice.

"Believe me, she is the ringleader. Don't trust her for—"

Dominique pulls the trigger, and the crack of the weapon is soaked up by the dense snowfall. Gerard cries out and flops back like a caught fish thrown onto the deck of a fishing boat.

"Follow me," Dominique says, and pushes off into the storm.

You don't. You can't leave Gerard lying there without trying to help, regardless of who or what he might be. A quick examination reveals that he is wounded, not dead. The bullet entered his right shoulder, probably smashing the collarbone and the rotator cuff of his shoulder. He moans and then tries to move to an upright position.

"She'll kill you. Don't trust her," he whispers.

Dominique appears out of the snow and fires two more shots at the supine Gerard. The bullets find their home. You stare at him, and then at her with horror.

"You wanted in, so you're in. If you don't like what you see, too bad. We do not play games here, and I suggest that you grow up very quickly, or else."

Turn to page 29.

You say a small prayer that you will reach the forests below. The trees should shelter you from the storm and give definition to the whiteness. You will be able to navigate down the slope and gain the safety of the town and the valley.

You promise yourself that when you get back to the Golf Hotel, you will immediately pack your bags and make tracks. This is not your idea of fun. But the memory of Uncle Gustav comes back quickly. Maybe you should stay and complete your assignment.

For now, you concentrate on the tricky descent. There are other ravines and sharp drops before you reach the security of the forests below. A fall, a twisted ankle, or a broken bone could spell disaster. No one would know where to look for you in this storm.

You trust your instinct, and with amazing good fortune, you reach the firs. Their giant branches are laden with fresh snow. You push on through what feels like a gigantic tunnel. Now and again a tree unloads its branches, and you are covered with snow. But you know that you will make it.

You feel your heart pumping strongly, and your breathing is good and steady. *Maybe I imagined that those people were after me,* you think.

Turn to page 73.

The information is staggering, and you are sworn to secrecy. Any leak of the names of persons involved could lead to worldwide instability. Plans to deal with the situation remain top secret. Problems in Japan and Italy have already made the worldwide situation difficult; public confidence in government in these nations has been shaken. People are frightened and cautious in many parts of the world.

A disturbing thought that nips at you is the idea that the people who appear to be helping you might well be connected with the strange group in the Golf Hotel. Nowhere in any newspaper or TV news show has there been mention of the capture, arrest, or indictment of the group. It is as if everything that happened to you was only a dream. Who knows? you say to yourself. Money can do strange things to people. Corruption goes up, down, and sideways.

The big issue is that the economies of the world's nations are so interconnected that pressure on one will result in pressure on another: it's like a huge hydraulic system. Nations, like people, are not isolated; they depend upon one another for survival and growth, and can in turn cause disaster for one another. You wonder which way it will all end.

The End

104

You are made to haul Gerard's body off the track and cover him with snow. It is a poor grave, and you mumble a few words to send him on his way.

Slowly your party of three heads back up the track, now covered with new snow. The best you can hope for is time and luck.

"You know, my young friend, wisdom would dictate that you should be more cooperative with us. After all, you haven't even given us a chance," Chin Lee explains. "There could even be rewards beyond your most ambitious expectations. Think this over. But not for too long."

The route back to the mountain hut is difficult because of the snow, but at last you reach it. You try your best to remember all the details about Chin Lee from the files you reviewed. Maybe, just maybe, there is something in the files, some vital bit of information, that you could use as a bargaining tool. You scrape your memory.

Arte Funk is nowhere to be seen. It is as if Gerard and Arte were never part of the party to begin with. The strange white-haired man appears to be in command. A shiver of cold fear travels up your back; you can imagine what lies in store for you.

Turn to page 111.

"Don't move. We are arresting you for fraud, embezzlement, smuggling, and murder. Stand up . . . slowly . . . turn around . . . hands in the air."

What started out as a beautiful day has turned into the nightmare that has haunted you ever since you made your pact with the devil that snowy afternoon in Corvarra, Italy. You turned over information that led to safe-deposit boxes containing lists of people in Europe and Asia who were either corrupt or corruptible. In the hands of the authorities, these lists would have spelled disaster for the people mentioned; in other hands, those of Pascal, Chin Lee, and your aunt, they became the golden keys to control of governments, money, and other people.

You became a respected member of this contemptible mob, traveling throughout the world as a high-class messenger. Influence, threats, bribery, and darker things became standard operating procedures for you. Now it is all over. You knew it would end like this.

As the helicopter leaves your sun-washed estate on the almost perfect Greek island, you welcome the end of your dream/nightmare and its constant fear and worry.

The End

107

Before the guard at the door can reply, two men burst into the room. They both hold automatic weapons.

"Freeze!" one shouts.

Several of the men in the room reach for weapons in their jackets and are savagely cut down for their efforts. Two others succeed in hiding themselves behind the bar. They return fire. Siegfried grabs your arm and motions toward the side door.

You need no further prodding and bound for the door. It gives way easily to your push, and you and Siegfried are outside and running. The trouble is that Siegfried is no athlete. Despite being spurred by sheer terror, his speed is marginal. You could leave him, or you could push him into the doorway of a shop just to your right. No one is following you at this moment, but there's no time to dillydally.

If you decide to leave Siegfried and run for it, turn to page 78.

If you decide to stick with Siegfried, turn to page 59.

108

"I hope this storm is just one of those spring flashes that peters out," you say out loud to yourself.

"It will, don't worry," comes a response. The voice is female and French in accent.

You turn slowly around, not sure what to expect. The image of Dominique Pascal holding a flat black Beretta automatic in her hand flashes in your mind. But when you complete the turn, you see her standing there on her skis with a smile and no weapon.

"How did you get here?" you ask.

"Like you, on my skis, how else? But do not let us talk too much. Gerard will not be far behind. We must get out of here at once."

Barely does she finish the words when Muscles, now known as Gerard, appears in a splash of snow. Running on pure instinct, you throw a hockey-style block at him and catch him off balance. He slams to the ground in a pile of skis and poles.

"Get moving!" you shout as you pole off into the storm.

"I'm your ally, not your enemy," Gerard shouts.

"Pay no attention to him," Dominique exclaims. "He wants to kill you."

Turn to page 101.

"The heck with it," you say. "I'll just leave that gift outside the door. Who knows? It could be trouble."

With this decided, you turn to other things: more study of the reports, a careful review of the floor plan of the hotel, and a scrutiny of the skiing possibilities pictured on the map of the runs. You take a fifteen-minute nap to top this all off.

By early afternoon, you are ready to go back out onto the mountain. The snow has had a chance to soften up, and the surface could be excellent. Just to be safe, you sneak out of your room the back way—across your private terrace.

Outside, the sun is brilliant, and despite the hint of high winds aloft and the smudge of clouds from the south that might spell mountain storms the next day, this is a superb afternoon for skiing.

Instead of taking the big tram, which looks quite jammed, you head for the chairlifts that leave from the edge of town. There is almost no one riding them; the route is long, the towers high, and the drop from a chair at the worst point would certainly be fatal. But it's warm, and you like being outside instead of cooped up inside a crowded tram.

Stepping into your bindings, you catch a chair and are soon gliding soundlessly over the rising mountain, crossing ravines, gorges, and open snowfields. You reach in your pack for a small tube of sunscreen and dab your nose, cheeks, and forehead.

Turn to page 94.

110

"Shut your mouth. You display the brains of a maggot. It is not for you to question any of us. You will do what you are told or you will die. It is as simple as that. There is no real choice. There is no deal. I will tell you what to do."

Slowly the other man slides the zipper on the briefcase and slips a paper out. Without looking at it, he hands it to you. The tension in the cramped cab of the Sno-Cat is tangible. You read:

POWER OF ATTORNEY

I assign power of attorney in all matters, both financial and personal, to Luigi Solomento of Milan, Italy. I understand the implications of this act, I acknowledge that it is irrevocable, and I state that I am in complete control of all my faculties and of clear mind. I also acknowledge that I am not being coerced by any person, group, organization, or government.

Signed,

Turn to page 96.

Perhaps the most persuasive person of this group is Dominique Pascal. Being close to you in age, she slowly but convincingly argues that it would be foolish to kill you—a distinct possibility if you do not cooperate—when so much of your life still lies ahead. Plus, it would put their operation at a greater risk once officials discovered that Gustav Hendrikson's nephew had been murdered. There is also a hint, just a hint, that she too dislikes what is going on. Perhaps this young woman will be a secret ally.

You decide to play for time, to pretend to go along with them, to give them what they want. By morning you agree to go to your uncle's safe-deposit box and turn over all the papers inside it to the group. They are jubilant and anxious to get on their way at first light.

But as first light comes, so too arrives a sharp command from the leader of a powerful militia force that has surrounded the mountain hut during the early morning hours.

"I command all of you to come out with your hands up. Leave all weapons where they are." The voice is stentorian, and the accent sounds more German than Italian. "You will be given exactly five minutes to surrender, and no more!"

White-hair scurries frantically to the rear of the mountain hut. Moments later you hear a fantastic explosion, and the back portion of the hut vanishes in a puff of acrid smoke.

"Come out at once," screams the voice of the commander.

Turn to page 65.

Choosing a banana, you peel it and quickly chomp it down. You follow this with a chocolate-covered cherry.

Later that night, when you fall into a light sleep after a heavy dinner, your breathing begins to slow down. Your lungs struggle a bit, but you are unaware of it. The commands in your brain are upset, and your breathing slides to a stop.

The next morning your body is discovered. An autopsy report several days later attributes your death to natural causes.

Life in the Golf Hotel goes on without you.

The End

114

There is a side exit to the hotel, and you make a beeline for it. But when you emerge onto the street, a white-haired man stands smiling in front of a black Mercedes sedan that looks to be about a midfifties vintage. The door to the backseat is open.

"Get in," he says. He has an English accent and a quiet but commanding tone.

You seem to have no alternative and reluctantly enter the car. He closes the door, gets into the driver's seat, and says, "We will wait for your aunt and Reginald. Relax."

Turn to page 33.

116

"Very simple. You and I try to leave this town alive and make our way back to Trento. There we will have adequate protection—although the Meridians have far-reaching claws. There is no place that is truly safe."

"Siegfried—Pierro—what should I call you?"

"Siegfried will do."

"Okay, Siegfried. Let's get this straight. You want the list of names and the numbers of the secret bank accounts—right?"

"Exactly," he replies.

"Tell me what to do, and I'll do it, but let's get out of here. Oh—one more thing. How do I know that you are who you say you are?" *How can I believe anyone anymore?* you ask yourself.

"My friend, you will have to take it on faith. After all, what are your alternatives? Come now, let us go. I have a car out back. Hurry."

If you decide to trust Siegfried and leave with him in the car, turn to page 90.

If you decide he is an impostor and try to make a dash for it, turn to page 68.

ABOUT THE AUTHOR

R. A. MONTGOMERY is an educator and publisher. A graduate of Williams College, he also studied in graduate programs at Yale University and New York University. After serving in a variety of administrative capacities at Williston Academy and Columbia University, he co-founded Waitsfield Summer School in 1965. Following that, Montgomery helped found a research and development firm specializing in the development of educational programs. He worked for several years as a consultant to the Peace Corps in Washington, D.C., and West Africa. He is now both a writer and a publisher.

ABOUT THE ILLUSTRATOR

FRANK BOLLE studied at Pratt Institute. He has worked as an illustrator for many national magazines and now creates and draws cartoons for magazines as well. He has also worked in advertising and children's educational materials and has drawn and collaborated on several newspaper comic strips, including *Annie*. A native of Brooklyn Heights, New York, Mr. Bolle now works and lives in Westport, Connecticut.

CHOOSE YOUR OWN ADVENTURE®